W9-CBC-606

ROBERT F. KENNEDY, JR.'S
AMERICAN HEROES

ROBERT SMALLS: THE BOAT THIEF

Illustrations by
PATRICK FARICY

HYPERION BOOKS FOR CHILDREN
New York

An Imprint of Disney Book Group

ACKNOWLEDGMENTS

My gratitude to my extraordinarily talented researcher Brendan DeMelle, and to Mary Beth Postman who organizes my life so that I have time to read history and write books for children, and my assistant Lori Morash who can somehow read my chicken scratch, and to Donna Bray at Hyperion who helps to make this endeavor so fun.

This book is set in 14-point Andrade Pro.

Printed in Singapore

Reinforced binding

Library of Congress Cataloging-in-Publication Data on file.
ISBN 978-1-4231-0802-3

Visit www.hyperionbooksforchildren.com

To my friend John Lewis and the other old war
horses who never stop fighting for the noble
ideal of Robert Smalls's America

—*R.F.K., Jr.*

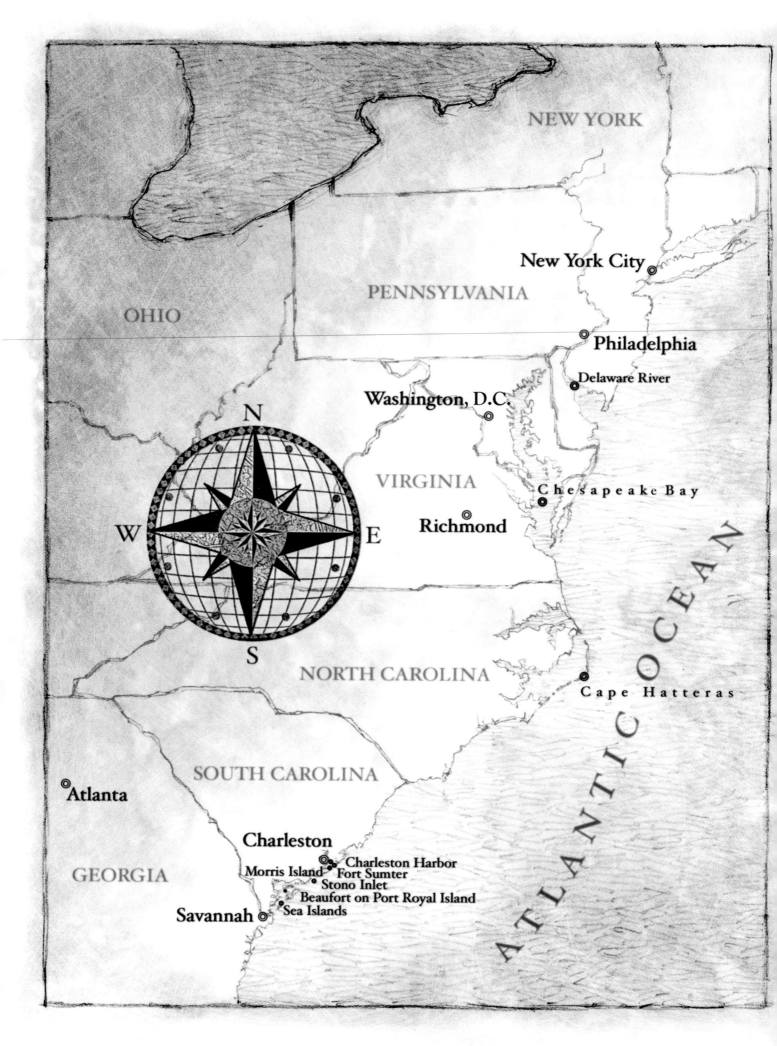

NEW YORK

New York City

PENNSYLVANIA

OHIO

Philadelphia

Delaware River

Washington, D.C.

VIRGINIA

Chesapeake Bay

N

Richmond

W   E

S

NORTH CAROLINA

Cape Hatteras

SOUTH CAROLINA

Atlanta

Charleston

Charleston Harbor

GEORGIA

Morris Island   Fort Sumter

Stono Inlet

Beaufort on Port Royal Island

Savannah   Sea Islands

ATLANTIC OCEAN

CONTENTS

INTRODUCTION

In the spring of 1862, the world was watching the South Carolina port of Charleston. One year before, the Confederate bombardment of Fort Sumter had launched the American Civil War. Confederate forces now occupied Fort Sumter and the many fortified islands that guarded the Rebel harbor. The Union forces had enjoyed very little in the way of good news since the Confederate takeover of Charleston.

Then, on a moonlit May night, nine black slaves stole the Confederate commander's gunship as it lay tied to a wharf in front of Confederate headquarters in Charleston Harbor and delivered it to the American navy. The vessel, a giant side-wheel steamship called the *Planter,* was the fastest ship in the harbor. She was the pride of Charleston and the most important ship in the local Rebel fleet. The daring slaves had commandeered her from under the noses of twenty-one Confederate troops guarding her from just a few feet away.

The brassy getaway riveted world attention and enraged the Confederate government. The loss of their finest ship, with its load of irreplaceable cannons and ordinance, was a terrible blow to the Rebel cause. But, even worse, the audacious and intricately coordinated escape exploded the Confederate claim that Southern slaves did not crave freedom and were incapable of decisive and deliberate action.

The saga of courage at the birthplace of the Civil War electrified Northern states weary of disastrous reports from the battlefield. The *New York Times* proclaimed the noble feat "one of the most heroic acts of the war." Northern papers praised "the plucky Africans" for their gallantry. They acclaimed the plot's ringleader—a illiterate slave pilot named Robert Smalls—as a national hero. Smalls, they said, had proven that black slaves were ready for full freedom and citizenship. The *New York Daily Tribune* asked, "What white man has made a bolder dash or won a richer prize in the teeth of such perils during the war?" The paper concluded that Smalls's actions had shown that "Negro slaves have skill and courage. They will risk their lives for liberty."

The daring adventure shattered widespread stereotypes about African slaves and inspired the broad public support that encouraged President Abraham Lincoln to issue the Emancipation Proclamation, freeing the slaves and giving them full United States citizenship.

Both North and South were ravenous for every detail about this extraordinary slave, Robert Smalls, who had masterminded this magnificent escapade. This is his story.

1.

HOUSE SLAVE AND SAILOR

◆━━━━●━━━━◆

Robert Smalls was descended from slaves from the African tribes of Guinea. His mother, Lydia, was born on a rice plantation in the Sea Islands off the South Carolina coast. She endured brutal cruelties laboring as a field slave until she was brought by her owner, John K. McKee, to work in his home on Prince Street in Beaufort, a sleepy little city on Port Royal Island. Recognizing her high character, natural kindness, and sharp wit, McKee entrusted her with the care of his five children. At age forty-nine she bore her only child, Robert, in a slave cabin in the McKees' backyard. The McKees were among South Carolina's wealthiest citizens, and the family treated Robert well. When John McKee died in 1848, Robert and his mother became the property of John's eldest son, Henry.

Despite the comparative comfort of their lives as house slaves, Lydia always reminded Robert of the harsh conditions of her early existence. She instilled in him a longing for freedom and made sure that Robert never forgot the precariousness of his condition. She forced him to watch slaves being whipped in the streets of Beaufort. She took him to the Beaufort Armory,

where slaves were auctioned. Robert saw families divided and watched black people being bought and sold like animals, in leg shackles and neck irons.

When Robert was twelve, his master sent him to Charleston to hire himself out. Robert worked first as a hotel waiter, then as a lamplighter for the city. His reputation for being a hard worker landed him a job on the Charleston docks as a stevedore, mainly driving the hoisting horses that powered the cranes used to lift heavy objects in the shipyard. He quickly progressed to foreman. Recognizing Robert's energy and technical abilities, the shipyard owner soon promoted him to sailmaker and topsail rigger.

In the warmer months, Robert sailed the Sea Islands and the Georgia and Carolina coasts on a merchant schooner. He was soon navigating with such skill and confidence that he became known as one of the finest sailors in South Carolina, able to manage any kind of boat. Although illiterate, he learned to understand maps and charts. He studied the locations of channels, bars and reefs, and bays and inlets from Charleston to Savannah, Georgia, and memorized the currents and tides so that he had mastered all the elements of sailing.

Although his wages legally belonged to his master, at age eighteen, Robert negotiated with Henry McKee to keep anything he earned over fifteen dollars per month. His sixteen-dollar salary left him only one dollar a month for his own pocket. Robert earned extra money through petty deals and odd jobs—mainly buying and selling items on his coastal cruises.

In 1858, at age nineteen, Robert married Hannah Jones, a slave hotel maid owned by Samuel Kingman. Their daughter Elizabeth Lydia was born a year later. Since his baby daughter was also the property of Kingman, Robert bargained with the master to buy freedom for Elizabeth and Hannah for eight hundred dollars. By 1861, after nearly four years of hard work, Robert had earned seven hundred dollars, an enormous amount of money for a slave.

But then Lydia bore him a son, and Robert worried that the new baby meant that he'd now have to pay more to purchase his family's freedom. He began to think of escaping.

Robert Smalls had heard through the "slave telegraph" that his mother had been left behind with ten thousand other slaves on Port Royal when the Yankees had captured the island in November. She was now working as a cook in Beaufort for the Union army under Major General David Hunter, who was planning to give all these slaves their freedom. Robert was determined to move his whole family north.

2.

THE *PLANTER*

---◆---

A YEAR BEFORE, ROBERT HAD HIRED ON AS A SAILOR ON THE *PLANTER*, a high-pressure side-wheeler designed to haul cotton that was owned by Captain John Ferguson. A large ship, 147 feet long and 50 feet abeam, the *Planter*'s broad deck could carry a thousand troops and their gear. The *Planter*'s shallow five-foot draft made her ideal for transporting men and supplies through coastal South Carolina's labyrinth of estuaries, tributaries, and rivers. Ferguson had chartered the *Planter* and her civilian crew to the Confederate navy, which had outfitted her as a gunship with a cannon in the bow and a howitzer astern.

As Charleston prepared for the expected Yankee attack, the *Planter* played a critical role patrolling the harbor, charting and placing mines, and carrying troops and armaments to the outlying forts and batteries.

Robert hired on as a deckhand. His perfect knowledge of the bays and shoals persuaded the Confederate officers to promote him first to head crewman and then to ship's pilot.

One day, a slave sailor joked to Robert that they should steal the *Planter*.

Smalls hushed his friend, whispering that the idea was more than a joke, and ordered him to never again mention it aboard ship. After work, the two of them began feeling out the other black crew members: two engineers and four other sailors and deckhands. They decided not to include one of the slaves, another deckhand, who could not be trusted.

The slaves gathered late at night and planned their bold scheme by candlelight at Robert's house. They agreed to be ready at a moment's notice and left it to Robert to decide when to move, promising to obey his orders.

On some nights the *Planter*'s white officers would leave their ship in Smalls's care, moored to the wharf in front of Confederate headquarters tightly guarded by twenty-one marines. On the afternoon of May 12, 1862, Confederate soldiers and stevedores loaded the *Planter* with six heavy guns and several hundred pounds of ammunition for shipment to the harbor for-tifications. The guns included two magnificent cannons taken from the Union army following the surrender at Fort Sumter. Those Yankee guns were damaged during the fierce battle but had since been repaired. The Rebels would now deploy the big artillery pieces for their own cause. Thinking to himself that these weapons would make a fine gift for "Uncle Abe"—President Lincoln—Smalls deliberately slowed down the loading process so that the cargo could not be delivered that day.

At day's end, the *Planter*'s captain, his mate, and chief engineer announced that they were going ashore to spend the night. As they ambled down the gangplank, the captain ordered Robert to have the ship ready to shove off at 6 a.m. on the high tide. "Aye, aye, sir," Smalls replied. The moment they were out of sight, Smalls spread the word among his crew that this was their night.

The slaves sent messages to their wives and children. That evening, as

Charleston slept, two women and their little ones stole away from their masters' homes. Arriving at the port in the darkness, they hid aboard a merchant ship moored to a nearby dock under the care of a slave sailor who was a friend of Smalls's and who would join the adventure.

3.

SAILING TO FREEDOM

———•———

NONE OF THE SLAVES WOULD SLEEP THAT NIGHT. Around 3 a.m., Smalls silently broke into the officers' quarters to steal the broad-brimmed, straw Confederate captain's hat and the captain's uniform and pistols. The slaves all swore to one another that if they were caught, they would detonate the ship's explosives, sink the *Planter*, and die fighting.

Knowing the captain and mates might return as early as 5 a.m., they fired up the steam engines at 3:30. The roar seemed loud enough to waken the whole city. Thick smoke from the stacks swept down onto Charleston. A terrifying eternity passed as the eight men waited for the steam pressure to build, frightened that the howling, billowing turbines would alert the captain or cause someone to sound the fire alarms. They prayed that the armed Confederate guards who patrolled the wharf, expecting an early departure, would not sound the alert.

When the pressure was sufficient, Smalls ordered his men to loose the lines and raise the Confederate flag. Then he blew the *Planter*'s whistle to signal they were leaving the wharf. Smalls stood beside the wheelhouse

9

at the captain's post, wearing the captain's hat and uniform. He held his arms akimbo, imitating the captain's well-known posture. Shielded by darkness, the *Planter* steamed slowly across the harbor to the dock where the women and children were secretly stowed. As soon as they had climbed aboard, Smalls turned his ship and sailed leisurely seaward, passing six fortified Confederate checkpoints bristling with deadly guns, and sounding at each the prescribed coded signals, which Smalls knew by heart.

The tide was against them, and they did not reach Fort Sumter till daylight. As they passed the great fort, Smalls fetched up his collar and pulled the straw hat low to hide the black skin of his face. He pulled the rope, making two long whistles and a short jerk—the code for guard boats leaving the harbor. The officer on watch signaled to him to pass, and Robert, cool as ice, steamed at a crawl directly under Fort Sumter's steep stone walls and powerful cannons. In that moment of greatest peril, he prayed to himself, *"Lord, you brought Moses and the Israelites from slavery, safely across the Red Sea. Please carry your children now to the promised land of freedom!"*

As soon as she was beyond Sumter's guns, Smalls buried the *Planter*'s throttle and changed course, racing for the open sea and the blockades. Through the morning mist, Robert could see the silhouettes of ten warships from the federal blockade squadron on the horizon. He set course for the nearest federal gunboat. As the slaves made good their escape, Robert ordered his men to strike the Confederate colors and haul up a bedsheet he'd stripped off one of the bunks.

In the crow's nest on the federal frigate *Onward*, the lookout spotted the Confederate gunship coming at full speed toward them out of the fog, and sounded the alarm. Thinking it meant to ram them, the *Onward*'s captain, F. J. Nickerson, brought *Onward* about to meet the hostile attack with his broadside guns. Just as he was about to order a cannon barrage, a sailor shouted that the ship was flying a white flag, and Captain Nickerson instructed his gunners to hold their fire. He signaled the *Planter* to pull in astern.

Captain Nickerson saw a dashing young black man wearing a Rebel captain's hat, dressed elegantly in a white shirt and Confederate officer's waistcoat, leaning confidently against the *Planter*'s gunwale. Doffing his hat expansively, the handsome youth saluted and called to the captain, "Good morning, sir! I've brought you some of the old United States' guns."

In front of Smalls on the *Planter*'s deck, eight triumphant black men began cheering wildly. When Captain Nickerson boarded the *Planter*, the exultant crew engulfed him, pleading that he give them an American flag to raise above their prize.

The moment the Stars and Stripes were hoisted, five more black passengers emerged from the *Planter*'s hatches, two women and three children. Smalls's wife, Hannah, with tears of joy flowing down her cheeks, raised her infant son, Robert, in her arms and told him to gaze at the American flag. "It means freedom, child! Oh, Robert, it means freedom!"

Captain Nickerson greeted them cordially, and after hearing Robert Smalls's story, sent him to retell it to the blockade squadron commander, who decided to send the *Planter* with its crew of escaped slaves under Union commanders sixty miles up the coast to Port Royal, the headquarters of the Union army and fleet. Their families would go to Beaufort, where they would be safe for the remainder of the war.

4.

BACK ON SHORE

BACK IN CHARLESTON, THE CONFEDERATE COMMANDER, Brigadier General Roswell S. Ripley, was astonished that morning when his troops told him that the *Planter* had vanished from her berth directly in front of Ripley's head-quarters on the Charleston wharf.

The Confederate troops who had guarded the *Planter* that night said that they had seen her captain in his familiar straw hat standing at the rail in the dark-ness as the ship fired her engines at 3:30 a.m. and then steamed off, flying the Confederate flag. The guards were not surprised to see her go, since they had been told she was scheduled to sail early. They watched her land briefly at a dock across the harbor. Then her

whistle blew and she steamed unhurriedly toward Fort Sumter, where the officer in charge received her salute, and, thinking her on guard duty, signaled her to pass into the outer harbor. Only one of the *Planter*'s original crew of nine slaves remained ashore. He was questioned and genuinely seemed to know nothing. At first the Confederates found it unthinkable that slaves could have commandeered their finest vessel. General Ripley only accepted the shocking truth when, using a telescope, he frantically scanned the horizon and found the *Planter* anchored between two federal frigates out beyond the sandbars.

The Charleston press called the *Planter*'s loss "criminal negligence" and blamed its Confederate officers for "disgusting treachery" in allowing "one of the most shameful events of this or any other war." Fuming over the abduction in their capital, Richmond, Virginia, the Confederates' top general, Robert E. Lee, ordered swift punishment for the guilty parties. The ship's white captain and mates were court-martialed, fined, and imprisoned.

Tales of the daring abduction triggered weeks of celebration in Northern states. Congress passed and President Lincoln signed a bill awarding Smalls and his crew half the value of the ship. Calling Smalls's leadership "one of the coolest and most gallant naval acts of war," the navy's grateful commander, Admiral Samuel F. Du Pont, asked that a prize of $5,000 be awarded to Smalls and that $15,000 be split among the eight other men and two women who had played key roles in the conspiracy.

5.

THE BATTLE FOR STONO INLET

---◆---

WITH YANKEE OFFICERS ABOARD AND SMALLS ACTING AS PILOT, the *Planter* arrived at Union headquarters in Port Royal at 10:30 that evening. The Union fleet commander, Admiral Du Pont, was anxious to talk to Smalls.

After retelling his story, Smalls gave Admiral Du Pont a book he had managed to purloin, containing all the secret codes and signals of the Confederate navy. The Confederate code book allowed the blockade vessels to decipher the various signal flags that were raised by the Confederate forts and batteries across Charleston Harbor.

Even more important, Smalls had memorized the location, size, and power of Confederate fortifications throughout coastal South Carolina and the exact locations where the Confederates had placed their mines and torpedoes in the creeks and tributaries to foil Union attackers.

Best of all, Smalls knew in great detail the movements of all the Confederate soldiers and arms. He told Admiral Du Pont that the Rebel army had secretly abandoned its fortification, guarding the northern approach to Charleston at Stono Inlet. Admiral Du Pont recognized that this

information would allow the Union army to retake Charleston from the land.

The Union army, under Major General David Hunter, had been stalled at Port Royal mainly due to a lack of vessels needed to transport the army among the complex waterways of the Carolina coast. Du Pont sent a dispatch to General Hunter with Smalls's information about Stono Inlet. In his dispatch, he described Smalls as "a man of superior intelligence" and urged that Smalls's information be treated with utmost importance. Acting on Smalls's tip, General Hunter immediately began moving his army along the coast for a ground assault on Charleston. The *Planter* was a godsend to General Hunter. His army had been badly in need of a shallow-water ship. Here was the perfect craft for ferrying the army through the rivers and shoals of South Carolina's coastal archipelagos. Due to Smalls's intricate knowledge of the local waterways, General Hunter asked him to remain on as pilot.

Smalls steered troops up the coast for the Union navy and led three federal gunships across the Stono Inlet shoals, guiding the attack on the fort. His detailed knowledge of the sounds and rivers helped the Union army take Stono Inlet and establish Yankee fortifications there. The U.S. Navy secretary credited Smalls with making the victory possible.

Unfortunately, bureaucratic delays by the Union army prevented General Hunter from moving against Charleston. The stall gave the Rebels the chance to fortify new defenses for the city, and the Yankees dropped their planned assault for the moment. Nevertheless, the Union victory at Stono Inlet would be a turning point in the battle for Charleston, and Stono would be an important base in future operations.

6.

CAPTAIN ROBERT SMALLS

—•—

Despite the legislation signed by Lincoln, and the efforts by Admiral Du Pont to award Smalls and the *Planter*'s crew their fair reward of $20,000 for delivering the gunship, mean-spirited accountants in the Department of War, not wanting former slaves to receive such a "fortune," reduced the total payout to $4,500, with $1,400 going to Smalls.

If he felt bitter, Smalls never showed it. For the next three years he served the Union army with rare distinction. He piloted the *Planter* and other ships through seventeen naval battles, always displaying courage and daring. Each time he engaged the enemy, Smalls knew he risked far more than did the white sailors he fought alongside. He and his crew of former slaves faced brutal torture, maiming, and death, if they ever fell into the hands of the Confederates.

On April 7, 1863, the Union command gave Smalls the honor of piloting one of the world's first ironclads—the *Keokuk*—during the naval assault on Charleston. Although the Union attempt to recapture Fort Sumter failed, Smalls distinguished himself by displaying coolness in battle. When the fleet stalled with its flagship run aground, Smalls guided the *Keokuk* around the stranded ships for a direct attack on the fort. There he came under hot fire from the Confederate guns. Cannonade blasts struck the *Keokuk* ninety-six times, with nineteen shots at or below the waterline. A shell burst damaged Smalls's eyes and killed his first mate. Despite his injury, Smalls steered his crew to safety, unloading them to a rescue ship just minutes before the *Keokuk* sank upright.

In May 1863, Smalls was back on the *Planter*, piloting for a Yankee captain on a supply mission on the Kiawah River near Charleston. They were carrying ammunition to an isolated Union army division on Morris Island and bringing badly needed rations to the hungry troops. Within view of the Yankee soldiers, a Confederate warship ambushed the *Planter*, forcing her between three Confederate forts where Rebel gunners raked her with a withering crossfire from three sides. The fierce fusillade tore into the *Planter*'s smokestack and wheelhouse. Fire from short rounds splintered her deck. The screaming shells and smoke panicked the captain, who ordered Smalls to beach the *Planter* and surrender. But he refused the order, shouting, "Not by a damned sight will I beach this boat for you." As the captain ran below to hide, Smalls took command of the ship, sailing the *Planter* through the maelstrom of smoke and

hot lead safely to the Union battery. Thousands of Union troops, desperate for supplies, had watched her run the savage gauntlet. Now they awaited her, cheering wildly on the landing. Major General Quincy Gillmore boarded the tattered *Planter* and dismissed the captain for cowardice. Then he promoted Robert to captain on the spot, making Robert Smalls the first black captain of a United States vessel in the history of our nation. He served at that rank for the remainder of the war.

7.

ABE LINCOLN

Even as he was fighting in the Civil War, Robert played an important role in the emancipation of black slaves and improving the lot of African Americans during reconstruction.

In August 1862, at the request of General Hunter, Robert traveled to Washington, D.C., with the abolitionist leader Reverend Mansfield French. In Washington, Robert met with President Abraham Lincoln, his secretary of war, Edwin Stanton, and his treasury secretary, Salmon Chase, to urge them to arm the thousands of black slaves who had been abandoned by their masters when Port Royal's Rebel population fled before the Union army. With charm and eloquence, Smalls told the president that former slaves were anxious, able, and badly needed to protect the Union-occupied regions of the South from Rebel raiders. Lincoln was convinced, and Smalls returned to Port Royal with the president's permission to enlist 5,000 black men as soldiers in the Union army, shattering the color barrier that had kept blacks out of military service.

Robert was considered a prince by black freedmen, who greeted him as a hero everywhere he went. Despite his inability to read or write, he became an

articulate and charismatic public speaker. Abolitionists sent Robert on a speaking tour to raise money at black and white church meetings for the Union cause and to help the former slaves who were living in desperate poverty. In 1862, the black community of New York City gathered at Shiloh Church to present Robert with a massive gold medal struck in his honor. The medal showed a relief of Robert and the *Planter* in the port of Charleston and praised Smalls for his "heroism, love of liberty, and his patriotism." Deafening cheers practically blew the roof off the famous church when he appeared with his wife and his little son, Robert, to speak at the lectern. As always, he was noble and modest and spoke confidently for the cause of freedom.

In May of 1864, a convention of black freedmen and whites in Beaufort selected Robert as a delegate to the Republican National Convention, making him one of the first four black men to be chosen in such a capacity to a national-party convention. But Smalls was still preoccupied with fighting the war.

8.

PHILADELPHIA

———◆———

Robert's commander had sent him to Philadelphia to refit and overhaul the battle-battered *Planter*. Certain Union officers, who were jealous of Smalls's success and speedy promotions, conspired to have him ordered to personally sail the *Planter* north unassisted. They were confident that the illiterate former slave could never navigate the impossibly intricate channels and strong currents of Cape Hatteras, the Chesapeake Bay, and the Delaware River. He would founder his ship and be drummed out of the service, they thought. Smalls, however, was overjoyed by the challenge and made the trip in just three days, once again astonishing his doubters.

In Philadelphia, Robert supervised the *Planter*'s refitting. In his spare time, he worked hard learning to read and write, a privilege forbidden to slaves under the laws of South Carolina. Of the *Planter*'s six black crew members, only one, John Smalls (no relation to Robert), the engineer, was literate. When a reporter asked him how he had learned to read, he replied, "I stole it at night, sir."

Robert continued working to support newly freed slaves in the South. With his customary bravery and dignity, he also struck a blow for equality in Philadelphia. Returning home one rainy day from the shipyard, Robert and a friend had just taken their seats on a city streetcar when a conductor ordered him to move to make way for white passengers. The conductor explained that city laws prohibited black people from sitting in streetcars: Smalls and his friend must move to the streetcar's outside platform. Smalls, instead, disembarked and walked home in the rain. The humiliation of the hero of Charleston received national publicity. The public outcry helped eliminate the race laws in Philadelphia, which finally integrated its streetcars in 1867.

9.

HOME TO BEAUFORT

————◆————

By the winter of 1864, Smalls and the *Planter* were back in action, supporting General William Tecumseh Sherman in his march across the South. After Sherman's army conquered Atlanta and Savannah, Robert helped move Union troops up the coast into the Carolinas. The Yankees took Charleston on February 17, 1865.

When Charleston surrendered, Smalls escorted General Rufus B. Saxton into the city, where adoring mobs of cheering blacks greeted them. On the outskirts of the crowd, standing with a small group of whites, Smalls spotted his old boss, Captain John Ferguson, the *Planter*'s original owner. Pulling General Saxton through the crowd, Smalls introduced him to Captain Ferguson, a gesture that testified to his changed status and equality.

After the war, Smalls returned to Beaufort and, using his congressional prize money, he bought the old McKee estate where he had been born. He would live there for the rest of his life. Working hard, he became a successful businessman and acquired extensive property and buildings around Beaufort. But he devoted most of his energies to public service. He labored to build Beaufort and Port Royal into communities where both races could live together, prosper, and flourish. Robert joined the South Carolina Militia and was promoted to major general, the militia's top commander.

As militia commander, he distinguished himself by peacefully settling a violent strike by rice-field workers. He negotiated with the striking workers in Gullah, the language of the Sea Island slaves, which he had learned as a boy. Gullah was a mixture of West African languages with seventeenth-century English. The workers told him of their terrible mistreatment and the cruelty of the plantation owners, who used a payment system designed to return them to the status of slaves. Afterward, Robert kept his promise to the workers by persuading South Carolina's governor to pass laws making such mistreatment illegal.

Robert built the first public school in South Carolina and became the leading advocate for public school education across the state. He was one of the founders of the Republican Party in South Carolina. The Republican Party was beloved by the black freedmen and all who loved democracy. This was the party of Lincoln, which, in Smalls's words, had "unshackled the necks of four million human beings."

Robert was chosen as a delegate to help draft the state's constitution in 1868. The document integrated South Carolina and gave equal rights to all her citizens. He remained a friend to both the black and white people of Beaufort, and in 1868 they elected Robert to represent them in the South Carolina Legislature. They sent him to the state senate in 1870. And in 1874, Beaufort elected Robert Smalls as its United States congressman. He served five terms in the House of Representatives, longer than any black person until the 1950s.

While in the House he authored and passed a bill requiring equal rights for both races on trains. Prior to that law, blacks were often given the worst seats

or forced to stand. He also fought to integrate the armed services and allow women the right to vote. He used his political power to fight corruption and waste in government. He fought for fair elections. He battled to reform the tax system, which favored the rich and punished the poor. He used his personal wealth and political connections to provide jobs and care for many poor people, both black and white, including his former masters, the McKee family, who were now destitute, having fallen on hard times. For fifty years Robert Smalls was the most powerful black man in South Carolina and a fierce fighter for American democracy and for the rights of the poor, women, and people of all races.

10.
THE CONFEDERACY RISES AGAIN

Up until 1876, the civil rights of former slaves in the Southern states were protected by the Republican Party, which controlled Congress and the presidency. Most important among those rights was the right to vote. Since blacks outnumbered whites by nearly two to one in South Carolina, many black officials now held power in state and national government.

But former Confederates were determined to depose blacks of their new-found rights and restore the order of the prewar South. They controlled the Democratic Party across the South and, by 1876, began gaining power nationally. At the same time, the Republican Party began deserting the Southern freedmen. The industrial revolution was spreading, and large, powerful industrialists known as "robber barons" were using their wealth to gain control of both political parties. Tempted by that easy money, the Republican Party embraced the great corporations, abandoned its idealism, and left the freed slaves to the mercy of their former masters.

The old-guard Confederates now busied themselves reversing many of the reforms that Robert Smalls had helped win for his fellow freedmen. White supremacist Democrats openly stole elections and threw out most of South Carolina's black elected officials. Lynchings and beatings designed to keep blacks from voting became a daily occurrence. Wholesale voter fraud marred nearly every election in the state. "We stuffed the ballot boxes," South Carolina Senator and former governor Ben Tillman would later boast to the United States Senate in 1900. "We shot Negroes; we are not ashamed of it!"

Beaufort, where blacks outnumbered whites seven to one, was one of the last remaining pockets of black political power. Because Robert also enjoyed the support of many of Beaufort's white residents, he was able to hold his seat long after the white supremacists had forced other black elected officials out of office. Nevertheless, Robert was under constant attack by the old Confederate guard, who still referred to him bitterly as "the boat thief." The Ku Klux Klan lynched Smalls's supporters, threatened his life and property, and turned every Election Day into a circus of violence, murder, and fraud designed to keep his supporters away from the polls.

In 1886, after Robert had served ten years in Congress, white supremacists from the old Confederacy finally stole the election from him.

Their allies in Congress, both Democrats and Republicans, who saw democracy and racial equality as "bad for business," prevented Robert from regaining his rightful seat. Robert's enemies also had him imprisoned on phony charges of taking bribes; Robert was pardoned by the governor and released from prison when those charges were proven false.

In 1895, Senator Ben Tillman called a state constitutional convention for the express purpose of robbing black South Carolinians of the right to vote by discarding the constitution that Smalls had helped to draft in 1868. Tillman meant to permanently make blacks second-class citizens.

Only six blacks attended the convention, all but one from Beaufort. Robert Smalls was their star. He delivered a series of extraordinary speeches

at the South Carolina Constitutional Convention in an unsuccessful attempt to prevent the disenfranchisement of blacks. Through breathtaking passion and intelligence, he nearly succeeded. His eloquent plea against bigotry and in support of America's promise of a truly representative democracy nearly persuaded even the hard-line white supremacists, who had solidified their control of the state. A contemporary writer called Smalls "a potent force in the convention.

"The ringing speeches made by him were masterpieces of impregnable logic, consecutive reasoning, bitter sarcasm, and fiery invectives. . . . His arguments were simply unanswerable, and the keenness of his wit, the cleverness of his arrangements, and the persistence with which he routed his opponents from one subterfuge to another astounded the convention."

But, in the end, Tillman and the forces of hatred were too powerful. Their new constitution robbed almost all of South Carolina's blacks of their right to vote and the other rights of American citizens. In South Carolina and across the South, those rights would not be regained until the civil rights movement of the 1960s.

Despite those setbacks, Robert Smalls refused to stop fighting for the principles of democracy and freedom. He campaigned across the country against South Carolina's unfair and undemocratic laws, always appealing to America's idealism, her decency, and sense of fairness. He remained committed and firm, devoted to the ideals of an America where men and women were treated fairly without regard to their race.

His noble character had won him many permanent friends, and he never relinquished his optimistic outlook. In 1890, he accepted an appointment from Republican president Benjamin Harrison as customs collector of the port of Beaufort. Robert held the post for twenty years. He managed the affairs of the customs office cleanly and professionally and left an impeccable record of honesty and good management. In 1900, Congress finally gave him the additional $5,000 that was his rightful reward for capturing the *Planter*. In 1913, Democrats took the White House and fired him from the customs-office job. He left without bitterness. Robert died two years later in 1915 and went before his maker beloved by his fellow citizens. His funeral was the largest in the history of the city. Thousands of grieving South Carolinians openly wept as a black chorus sang Robert's favorite spiritual, "Shall We Meet Beyond the River."

AFTERWORD

ROBERT SMALLS WAS A TRUE AMERICAN PATRIOT. Despite the burdens America had laid upon him, he loved our country. He believed in the "inherent justice" of American democracy and in the principles espoused in the Declaration of Independence. To him the American dream meant building a nation that was a praiseworthy example to all humanity and reflected the best of the human character.

He played an important role in making America a true representative democracy for the first time in her history. Thanks in part to his efforts, between 1865 and 1876, for a brief shining moment, America came close to achieving its promise.

In 1876, that America, which seemed so much within reach during the decade after the Civil War, was eclipsed by the forces of ignorance, hatred, and greed. Always optimistic about human decency, Smalls was a practical realist who knew that democracy and freedom had to be fought for and cherished and could never be taken for granted. His life was a noble, dignified, and courageous struggle for those ideals, a struggle that only ended on the day he died.

But Smalls's spirit rose again fifty years later to invigorate and inspire the souls and voices of a new generation of black leaders like Martin Luther King, Jr., who would finally guide America toward keeping its great covenant with humanity and history.

BIBLIOGRAPHY

BOOKS

Billingsley, Andrew. *Yearning to Breathe Free: Robert Smalls of South Carolina and His Families.* Columbia, S.C.: University of South Carolina Press, 2007.

Brown, Susan T. *Robert Smalls Sails to Freedom.* Minneapolis: Millbrook Press, 2005. (written for young people)

Cooper, Michael L. *From Slave to Civil War Hero: The Life and Times of Robert Smalls.* New York: Dutton Juvenile, 1994. (written for young people)

Meriwether, Louise. *The Freedom Ship of Robert Smalls.* Englewood Cliffs: Prentice Hall, 1971. (written for young people)

Miller, Edward A. *Gullah Statesman: Robert Smalls from Slavery to Congress, 1839-1915.* Columbia, S.C.: University of South Carolina Press, 1995.

Sterling, Dorothy. *Captain of the* Planter: *The Story of Robert Smalls.* New York: Doubleday, 1958. (written for young people)

Uya, Okon Edet. *From Slavery to Public Service: Robert Smalls, 1839-1915.* New York, Oxford University Press, 1971.

ARTICLES

Harper's Weekly. "Robert Smalls: Captain of the Gun-Boat 'Planter,'" June 14, 1862. See http://www.sonofthesouth.net/leefoundation/civil-war/1862/june/robert-smalls-planter.htm